It was a dream come true...

Was she really hearing this? Had Tommy Weaver actually asked her out on an honest-to-goodness date? What was she going to wear? How was she going to do her hair? Wait till she told Gibbler!

At that moment, Stephanie rushed downstairs with the CD. "I'm back," she said breathlessly. "Sorry I took so long."

D.J. stood back and gagged. "Stef, how many gallons of perfume did you put on while you were upstairs?"

"I just put on one little dab . . . from every bottle on your dresser." She turned to Tommy. "Can you please sign this? I'll treasure it forever."

"Sure," he said.

She watched with pounding heart as he signed her CD: "With all my love, Tommy."

FULL HOUSE

KISS A FROG, PRINCESS

by Bonnie Worth
Based on the series *FULL HOUSE*™ *created by*
Jeff Franklin

and on episodes written by
Marc Warren & Dennis Rinsler
Stacey Hur
Diana "Jennie" Ayers & Susan Sebastian

A PARACHUTE PRESS BOOK

Parachute Press, Inc.
156 Fifth Avenue
New York, NY 10010

ISBN: 0-938753-63-0
Printed in the United States of America
September 1992
10 9 8 7 6 5 4 3 2 1

ONE

D.J. Tanner and her best friend, Kimmy Gibbler, had just returned from their usual Friday afternoon at the mall. Walking into D.J.'s bedroom, they threw their shopping bags on the bed.

Kimmy went over to the dressing table to try on her new glow-in-the-dark eye shadow. But what was this?

The mascara wand was out of its case, and a pink film of blusher powder lay all over the mirrored tabletop. The lids were off all the

1

eye shadow pots, too. "Don't look now, Deej," said Kimmy, "but somebody's been using your makeup again."

D.J. looked annoyed. "It's probably Michelle. I told her to stay out of my stuff, but I guess she can't resist."

Lately, five-year-old Michelle had been raiding D.J.'s makeup collection. She liked to paint her face like a crown princess, though *clown* princess was more like it.

D.J. had only recently gotten her own room, which had once been her uncle Jesse's. Before that, she had shared one with her nine-year-old sister, Stephanie.

It wasn't easy to find privacy in such a crowded household. Uncle Jesse and Danny's best friend Joey had moved in after the girls' mother died, when Michelle was only a baby. Later came Rebecca, and then Alex and Nicky—Uncle Jesse and Rebecca's twin baby boys. Now that Uncle Jesse's family lived up in the attic, and Joey lived down in the basement, and Danny and the three girls lived in between, the house was fuller than ever. It was also more fun than ever—most of the time.

"*Petunia* . . ." said Stephanie, walking into the room, "*p-e-t-u-n-i-a.*" For the past hour, Stephanie had been pacing back and forth in her own bedroom, practicing her spelling. The fourth-grade spelling bee was only five days away.

"Stephanie, you can't just walk in here," said D.J., who was standing in front of the mirror. "You have to knock."

"Sorry," said Stephanie. She went back to the door, knocked, and then walked in again. "How was the mall?"

D.J. turned away from the mirror and looked at her younger sister, who was wearing a pair of lime-green bicycle shorts and a silver-sequined halter top—both of which were D.J.'s. She was also wearing D.J.'s makeup—*all* over her face. *So Michelle isn't the culprit, after all,* D.J. thought.

D.J. and Kimmy stared at Stephanie.

"What are you guys looking at?" Stephanie asked innocently.

"Your face," D.J. said flatly. "And *my* outfit. Stephanie, how many times have I told you that I don't want you in my room when I'm not here?"

3

Stephanie counted on her fingers in an exaggerated way. "Maybe five times in the last week and a half? I'm sorry Deej, but I'm trying to figure out what to wear to my birthday party on Tuesday. A girl needs to experiment now and then."

"You and Dr. Frankenstein," D.J. said. "Well, do me a favor and experiment when I'm home from now on, okay?"

"Yes, sister dear. So what did you get at the mall? My birthday present?" Stephanie asked hopefully.

"Are you kidding?" Kimmy said in her usual cheery voice. "No way." She went over to her shopping bag and whipped out the day's prize purchase—a superlong, platinum-blond, 100 percent acrylic wig. "This was on sale. Half price."

Kimmy tried it on. "Well? Do I win the Marilyn Monroe look-alike contest, or what?" she asked, batting her eyelashes.

"You look more like a contender for the Comet look-alike contest," Stephanie told her. "No offense, Comet," she added to the family dog, who had just wandered into the room.

4

She gave him an affectionate scratch behind his ears.

"Oh, Stef!" said Kimmy, not paying any attention to the insult. "You'll never guess who we saw at the mall. Jimmy Fanelli!"

"Who cares?" Stephanie scoffed. "Timmy Fanelli is twice as cute as Jimmy Fanelli."

"No way, squirt," said Kimmy. "Jimmy Fanelli is three times cuter than Timmy Fanelli."

"Timmy Fanelli is definitely cuter," insisted Stephanie.

"Jimmy Fanelli," said Kimmy, putting the wig on Stephanie's head. "Not bad." The wig was the same color as Stephanie's real blond hair but about ten times thicker.

Stephanie placed the wig back on Kimmy's head. "Timmy."

"Jimmy."

"Timmy."

"D.J., tell your little sister she doesn't know what she's talking about," said Kimmy.

D.J., who had been busy cleaning up her dressing table, turned to her best friend and her sister.

"Why are you guys arguing?" she asked. "Timmy and Jimmy are identical twins!"

"Jimmy's two minutes older. He's much more mature," Kimmy said stubbornly, walking over to the mirror. "Two-tone," she said, admiring the effect of her auburn curls poking out from the top of the blond wig. "Radical!"

"That's the dumbest thing I've ever heard," Stephanie said.

"Let me get this straight." Kimmy faced Stephanie, hands on hips. "*You* are calling *me* dumb?"

"Gibbler, you're so dumb you don't know how dumb you are."

"I know how dumb *I* am," said Kimmy. "You're the one who's dumb, Stephanie. Capital *d-u-m—Dumb*."

"Kimmy," D.J. pointed out, "there's a *b*."

Kimmy jumped and began swatting at herself. "Bee? Where? I hate bees."

D.J. grinned. "I think we have a winner," she said. "Anyway, I don't know why you two are arguing about the Fanelli twins. If what Kimmy says is true, we're about to meet a guy who's ninety million times cuter than both Fanellis rolled into one."

"Who?" said Stephanie.

"Tommy Weaver!" cried D.J. and Kimmy at the same time.

Tommy Weaver, America's number-one teenage rock star was actually going to be a guest on Danny Tanner's local TV show, *Wake Up, San Francisco*. At least that was what Kimmy said. Kimmy had overslept that morning. While she waited for her mom to drive her to school, she had seen part of the show—the part where Danny'd announced his upcoming guests.

"Tommy Weaver!" cried Stephanie. "Where? When? How?"

"He's going to be on Dad's show next week," said D.J.

"I don't get it," Stephanie said. "I mean, Tommy's song has been number one on the charts for the past six weeks. He's incredibly hot. *Everybody* must want Tommy! How did our dad, wonderful as he is, get him to come on his inky-dinky little show?"

"Tommy's cousin produces Dad's inky-dinky show," D.J. explained. "That's how he got him."

Just then, they heard a car door slam.

"Dad's home!" D.J. and Stephanie screamed, sprinting toward the stairs.

TWO

From the front porch, Danny Tanner could hear his daughters' feet thundering on the stairs. He smiled, pleased to think his girls couldn't wait to welcome him home from a hard day at the studio.

"Dad! Dad!"

Stephanie and D.J. came running toward him, while their little sister, Michelle, darted in from the kitchen. She wore a glittering crown and carried a pink fairy-princess wand to match her sneakers and her tutu.

"Oh, look," Danny said, "here come all

9

three of them. They can't wait to hug their dad." He held his arms out to them.

"Is it true, Dad?" said Stephanie, not noticing his outstretched arms. She couldn't wait to find out if Tommy Weaver would really be on her dad's show.

On most days, Michelle would leap into her father's arms—but not today. Today she wasn't smiling her usual smile either. She pointed her wand at Stephanie. "She hid my Frog Prince tape!"

"After the hundredth time you played it," said Stephanie rolling her eyes.

"I was trying to learn all the words," Michelle said.

"I was trying to forget them," said Stephanie. "And I was trying to study for the fourth-grade spelling bee next Wednesday."

"Everybody knows bees can't spell," Michelle pointed out.

"Guess I can put my arms down now," their father said sadly. No one seemed to be in a hugging mood.

"So, Dad," D.J. said eagerly, "*is* it true?"

Danny took off his jacket and hung it up in the closet.

"Is what true, Deej?" he asked, wiping some dust from the closet door. Danny Tanner was the neatest father on the block—maybe in the whole country.

"What you said on the show this morning," D.J. said. "Kimmy saw part of your show this morning. Is what you announced today true?"

Danny tried to look innocent. "That Telegraph Hill affords a spectacular view of the sights of San Francisco on fog-free days?" he asked. "Yes, I'd say it's true."

D.J. gave her father a look. "You know perfectly well what I'm talking about, Dad. I'm talking about Tommy Weaver. Is it true he's going to be your guest host . . . all next week?"

Danny nodded.

Stephanie shrieked. "Tommy Weaver! Why didn't you tell us! I mean, this is big, big news. I'm talking large, I'm talking huge, I'm talking massively gigundo."

"You're talking too much," Michelle said. "Who is this Tommy person anyway? If he's not the Frog Prince, he's just another rock-and-roller to me."

"Go kiss a frog, Princess," Stephanie told her little sister. "He's not just any rock-and-roller. His poster's hanging over my bed. He's the last thing I see before I fall asleep—except the inside of my eyelids, of course."

Danny smiled. For once, his daughters were showing an interest in his show. Usually they couldn't care less about his guests. But usually he didn't invite teenage-heartthrob superstars.

"So, Dad, when can I meet him?" Stephanie said.

D.J. pushed herself forward. "Never mind her, Dad. When can *I* meet him?"

"I'm sure he'd much rather meet me," said Stephanie. "After all, the man likes intelligent conversation. He'll want a girl capable of conversing on a number of subjects. A girl who can spell. A girl who—"

"Thinks lime-green bicycle shorts go with sequined halters? Think again!" D.J. said.

"Girls! Girls!" Danny held up his hands. "I'm not sure I'll be able to introduce either one of you to Tommy Weaver."

The girls fell silent and stared at him in horror.

"Look, girls, I haven't even met the guy

yet. For all I know, he might not even sign autographs, much less agree to meet the daughters of his host. You know how some of these superstars can be. But I promise I'll bring home tapes of the week's shows."

"Dad," D.J. said gently. "Relax. Tommy happens to be one of the nicest rock stars ever born. All the fan magazines say so. I'm sure he'll sign autographs and be happy to meet us. . . . " She gave her sister a look. "I mean *me*. I doubt very much that he has any interest in, or time for, mere children."

Stephanie swelled with anger. "You want to bet? I bet you can't even spell the word *autograph. Autograph: a-u-t-o-g-r-a-p-h.*"

"Oh yeah? How about *g-e-t l-o-s-t.*"

"Girls! Girls!" Danny spoke over their shouting. "Are these really the Tanner girls I'm hearing? Those loving sisters, scrapping over a boy? Actually competing?"

"Chill out, Mr. T.," said Kimmy, coming downstairs in the long blond wig, which she'd arranged beauty-queen style to fall over one shoulder.

"Never fear, the tie-breaker is here," Kimmy said, batting inch-long false eyelashes

13

at Danny. "Get me a date with Tommy Weaver and I guarantee you the sisterly competition will be over. Advantage: Gibbler."

Danny raised his eyes to the ceiling. "Tommy? Wherever you are, I'm truly sorry."

THREE

D.J. and Kimmy spent Sunday night giving each other make-overs. They were now on the sixth make-over of the weekend. Ever since Friday, when they'd gotten the news about Tommy Weaver, they had been trying out all kinds of new looks. The room looked as if a tornado had recently whipped through it.

The closet doors were flung open wide. Half the clothes had been yanked out and were draped over the backs of chairs. The dressing table, the desk, the counters, the windowsills, and every other available surface was littered with tubes of makeup and pots of cream.

Both girls were lying on D.J.'s twin beds, with cucumber slices over their eyes and green glop on their faces. D.J.'s wet hair was wrapped in a towel. Kimmy's hair was set in large rollers. On the table between them was a bowl with a special red hair-rinse mixture that D.J. had prepared for Kimmy.

From across the room, the tape deck played Tommy Weaver's latest album. They sang along with it until Kimmy said, "I think my avocado mask is hardening. What about yours?"

D.J. reached up and touched her mask. It felt hard and crackly. "Yeah, I'm turning into guacamole myself."

"Mmmmmm . . ." said Kimmy, "let's scrape it off with corn chips."

"Can't," D.J. said. "I'm on a diet for Tommy."

Just then, a new song came on.

"Oooo, I love this song!" Kimmy said.

16

"Me, too," D.J. agreed. "When the song is over, we can take off the masks. Then I'll comb out your perm and give it the special rinse."

D.J. got up and felt her way over to the tape player to pump up the volume. Her chin was pointed toward the ceiling so as not to disturb the cucumbers. Then she felt her way back to her bed again. She sighed deeply as Tommy began to sing again.

The two girls were so focused on Tommy's singing that they didn't hear Michelle come into the room. She had come to tell them that Uncle Jesse was baking gingerbread cookies.

Michelle took one look at D.J. and Kimmy and figured they had already eaten. Their faces were smeared with avocado goo and their eyes were covered with cucumber slices. *And they say* I'm *a messy eater*, Michelle thought.

She wandered over to the table and peered into the bowl of red hair rinse. Next to the bowl was a red plastic bottle, which caught her eye. She picked it up and squeezed. Some red goop oozed out of the top. She squeezed again and squirted a big glob of red goop into

17

the bowl. There! Now the mixture was an even darker red.

Michelle looked at D.J. and Kimmy, who seemed to be off in dreamland. She was about to touch the green stuff on D.J.'s face—lightly so she wouldn't wake her—when the aroma of gingerbread filled the room. *They can have cookies when they wake up*, she thought, tiptoeing out of the room. *But only if they promise to wash their faces.*

"What if he can't do it?" D.J. spoke up after the song was over.

"What if *who* can't do *what*?" Kimmy asked.

"What if my dad can't pull the strings he needs to get us to meet Tommy?"

"Simple," Kimmy said, "you disinherit him."

"What do you mean?" said D.J. "When you disinherit someone, it means you don't leave them your money. I don't have any money."

"You will when you become Mrs. Tommy Weaver—unless I become her first. You'll be rich. Then you can disinherit your father."

D.J. was silent for a moment, trying to

figure out the Gibbler way of thinking. Kimmy always seemed to have an answer to everything—even if it didn't exactly make sense.

"Kimmy, how can I become Mrs. Tommy Weaver if my dad never introduces us in the first place?"

"Good point," said Kimmy. "If you're smart enough to figure that out, then you're smart enough to figure out how we can meet Tommy."

"Well, as a matter of fact, I *have* thought of one way."

"How?" Kimmy reached up and felt the rollers to see if they were dry yet. Almost. She couldn't wait for D.J. to put on the rinse.

"Well, as you know, it's Stephanie's tenth birthday Tuesday," D.J. said.

"Uh-huh," said Kimmy. "She wants me to get her a Tommy Weaver sweatshirt. Like she doesn't already own four!"

"Yeah, but I think she'd rather get Tommy Weaver himself," D.J. said.

Kimmy sat up so fast the cucumber slices fell into her lap. "What are you talking about, Deej?"

"I'm talking about killing two birds with one stone. You know how my dad's been really stumped about what to do for Stephanie's birthday this year? I mean, she's getting too old for clowns. Too old for toys, too. What if I suggest to my dad that he get Tommy Weaver to make a personal appearance at Stephanie's birthday party?"

"I don't get it. Why would you give the World's Biggest Hunk away to your little sister? Don't we want him for ourselves?"

"Of course we do. But Stephanie's a mere child. Naturally, he'll be more interested in a woman like me . . . I mean, us."

Kimmy nodded, beginning to like the idea. "Tommy Weaver, the ultimate guy! Every girl's birthday wish come true! But will your dad go for it?"

"He should. You know how he'd do anything to make sure we have happy birthdays. If I tell him that this is the one and only present that will make Stef happy, then he'll perform miracles to make sure it happens."

"Tanner, you are truly a genius," said Kimmy. "And now, what about my rinse?"

D.J. sat up and removed her cucumber

slices. The bright lights made her blink for a few seconds. Then she got up and went to get the bowl.

"First, I'll apply the rinse. Then you'll have to sit under the hair dryer. I hope you like the color I mixed for you. It's very subtle. Shimmering Peach."

"Thanks, Deej. I wouldn't trust my hair to anyone but you."

"Kimmy, you can't *afford* anyone but me."

FOUR

Down in the kitchen, Jesse had just finished frosting a tray of gingerbread men. He passed it under the twins' noses. From their twin baby seats, they tried to reach for the tray with their chubby fists. But Jesse held it just out of their reach.

"Mmmmm . . . Daddy's cookies. At times like this, I'll bet you little guys wish you had teeth."

A moment later, Michelle came downstairs and announced, "D.J. and Kimmy have green food smeared all over their faces."

"That isn't food," Rebecca said, laughing. "At least not for eating. That's food for beauty. Those are beauty masks. When you put certain kinds of food on your face, it can help make your skin smoother and healthier-looking."

Michelle's eyes lit up. "Can I have a beauty mask made out of chocolate?"

"If you cover your face with chocolate, you won't be able to see this letter board, honey," Danny said. "It's time for your spelling lesson."

"Aw-*right!*" said Michelle. "Let's have a spelling bee."

"Okay, Michelle, this is an *a*," said Danny, pointing to the letter he had put on the magnetic letter board. Both D.J. and Stephanie had learned their alphabet on that same board.

"I know!" Michelle said, swinging her legs. "*A* is for *apple*."

Danny nodded, "Yes, Michelle, that's right. But I have a little system that really makes learning fun. *A* is for *Ajax*, *b* is for *Brillo*, *c* is for *Clorox*." He picked up each letter from a cardboard tray.

"*C* is for *cookie*, you mean," Michelle said. She reached out, grabbed a gingerbread man off the tray, and bit its head off. The cookie was still very warm—just the way she liked them.

Danny picked up a *d*. "*D* is for *disappointment*," he said before he could stop himself.

"*Disappointment?*" asked Michelle, puzzled.

"*Disappointment*," Danny said sadly, turning to Rebecca. "It's what D.J. and Stef are going to feel if I can't introduce them to Tommy Weaver."

Danny often found himself looking to Rebecca for advice on problems that needed a woman's touch.

"Oh, don't give up so fast, Danny," said Rebecca. "If *you* can't get him to meet them, maybe *I* can." Rebecca worked with Danny as his co-host on *Wake Up, San Francisco*.

"I'm not sure that's such a good idea, Becky."

"Besides," she said, "what's the big deal?

It's your show. Invite the girls onto the set after the taping. Tommy won't mind."

"That's the thing of it," Danny admitted. "*I* might mind."

"You? I don't understand."

"Those girls are so obsessed with Tommy Weaver," said Danny, "that it's like some kind of sickness. I can't imagine what they'll do if they meet him in person."

"I don't know. I once had a terrific crush on a rock star," Rebecca said.

"And who was this?" Jesse asked, pretending to be jealous. He was in the middle of giving his sons their first taste of crushed-up cookie.

"Oh, he wasn't anybody famous. Just the lead singer in a local band that played at all the town dances. Gary and the Hayseeds!" Rebecca sighed and got a faraway look in her eyes. "Gary was my heartthrob."

"Hunka hunka hayseed! Have mercy!" Jesse said.

"I had pictures of him on my wall, tapes of his music . . . I was really in love with that guy."

"Then what happened?" Jesse asked.

"My uncle Bob got me a backstage pass to meet him in person. When I discovered he had bad breath and pimples, my crush was crushed." Rebecca looked at Danny. "So cheer up," she said. "Maybe Tommy Weaver will prove to be a dud, too, and the girls will get back to their lives."

Just then, Stephanie came through the swinging door. "It's gone, gone, gone!" she said.

"What's gone?" Danny asked.

"My brain. The spelling bee's this Wednesday and I can't remember how to spell *success*. How many *c*'s and how many *s*'s? And where the heck do they go? I'm doomed!"

Danny said, "Now, Steph, get a grip. You're a winner, remember? All you need is a mnemonic device."

"What the heck is a knee monic device?" Stephanie asked. "My brain needs help, not my *knee*."

"It's one word, Steph," said Danny. "*Mnemonic*."

"But what does it mean?" Stephanie asked impatiently.

"If it's Dad's idea, it must be for cleaning," Michelle said, taking a bite of her cookie.

"It's a little trick to help you remember certain words. Take the word *success*. 'Double the *c* and double the *s* and you'll always have success.' Get it?"

Stephanie nodded slowly. "Double the *c*, double the *s: s-u-c-c-e-s-s . . . success!*"

"And you can make up a mnemonic device for any word you have trouble with," Danny said.

Stephanie brightened. "Davey Chu's gonna wish he never learned the alphabet." Davey Chu, one of the four top spellers in the fourth grade, was Stephanie's stiffest competition.

"I can spell *alphabet*," Michelle said, as her sister ran back to the living room to study. Then she sang, "*A, b, c, d, e, f, g, h, i, j, k, l, m, n, o, p, q, r, s, t, u, v, w, x, y,* and *z*. Now I know my ABCs, next time won't you sing with me?'"

Danny smiled patiently. "Well, the word

alphabet's in there someplace. Now," he said, picking up the alphabet tray, "where were we? Oh, yes, *d* is for *Drano.*"

Just then, D.J. and Kimmy came down the kitchen stairs.

"Well?" Kimmy asked everyone. "How do I look?"

The grown-ups stared in silence.

Kimmy obviously hadn't looked in the mirror yet. Nobody there wanted to be the one to tell her the truth.

"Isn't it cute?" said D.J., looking guilty and terrified all at once. "*Isn't* it cute, everybody?" she asked hopefully.

No one said a word. They just continued to stare at Kimmy's hair in shock.

Finally Michelle said, "You look like Bozo the clown!"

D.J. winced. Her little sister was right. Kimmy's hair looked like one bright red frizz ball. What had happened? She had mixed the rinse so carefully. Shimmering Peach was supposed to be subtle—but subtle it wasn't. The rinse should have been called Flame Broiled.

"So you're pleased with your work?"

Kimmy turned to D.J.

"Oh, it's more than I ever thought it would be." D.J. tried her best to sound honest, but she couldn't look Kimmy in the eye.

"And I look stunning?"

D.J. nodded. "I'm definitely stunned."

"I think you'd better take a look in the mirror," Rebecca said gently.

"Kimmy, don't!" D.J. cried out. Kimmy was going to be furious!

"She's got to know the truth sooner or later," Rebecca said. She led Kimmy over to the kitchen wall mirror and stood back, biting her lip.

Kimmy looked in the mirror. "Ohmigosh!" she cried. Her hand flew to her mouth.

"Kimmy, I am so sorry," D.J. said. "I'll pay to have it shaved."

"Are you kidding?" Kimmy turned away from the mirror, a huge grin spreading across her face. "I love it! I'm finally on the cutting edge of fashion. And the best part is"—she fluffed her hair out and did a dramatic turn, like a model on the runway—"Tommy's gonna love it!"

FIVE

"Can I lick the spatula?" Michelle asked, her mouth watering.

"Not yet," Rebecca said as she frosted the top of the triple-layer mocha fudge cake. It was the morning of Stephanie's birthday, and while the older girls were upstairs getting ready for school, Michelle was in the kitchen with Rebecca, "helping" to frost Stephanie's birthday cake.

30

"*Now* can I lick the spatula?" Michelle asked two seconds later.

"Soon," said Rebecca. "Stephanie's cake has to be perfect. Keep frosting."

A few more seconds passed. "*Now* can I lick the spatula?"

Rebecca gave in. "Yes! Now you can lick the spatula."

"It's about time!" With the spatula, Michelle took a huge scoop of frosting out of the bowl and began to lick it.

"Michelle! Look what you've done! Now I don't have enough to finish the cake. I'll have to make more."

"Gee," said Michelle, her mouth full, "that's too bad!"

As Stephanie dragged herself downstairs, she didn't exactly look the part of the birthday girl. She looked pretty gloomy.

Yesterday, she had been disappointed when her father came home without Tommy Weaver's autograph. But Danny'd said he couldn't find a pen that worked. What a lame excuse! It seemed as if he didn't *want* her to get Tommy's autograph.

"C'mon, Dad," Stephanie pleaded this morning. "Please take me to your show today. I just have to meet Tommy Weaver."

"Sweetheart," Danny said gently. "I'll try to get his autograph today, I promise, but you cannot miss school just because some rock star's on my show. I'll bring home a tape of the show."

"I want to meet him in person. Today is my tenth birthday—the big one-oh. Dad, I can't believe you wouldn't let your own daughter meet her all-time favorite singer in the whole universe on her birthday. And I thought you loved me." Stephanie swallowed hard over the lump in her throat.

D.J. applauded. "Great guilt trip."

"Thank you," Stephanie said somberly. She turned to her father and said, "Did it work?"

"No," he said.

"I knew I should've gone for some tears," she said as she went slowly out the door.

"Have fun at school," Danny called after her.

When Stephanie was gone, D.J. said, "Dad, that was pretty cold. I mean, it *is* her birthday and she *does* worship the guy. Didn't you even *ask* him?"

Danny smiled. "Deej, you've gotta keep this a secret. I did take your advice. I asked Tommy. He's turned out to be a really great guy. And he agreed to stop by Stef's party after school today."

D.J. screamed. Tommy Weaver! Under her very own roof! Her plan had worked! Wait till she told Kimmy. Kimmy would have a cow. She'd have a whole herd of cows! "Oh, Dad," D.J. said, throwing her arms around him. "You're unbelievable!"

He smiled modestly. "Yeah, I know. Am I the raddest, baddest dad a kid ever had?"

D.J. grinned at him. "You were until you said that."

SIX

The party started at three so that the guests could come straight from school. The gifts they brought made a small colorful mountain on the coffee table.

The living room was gaily decorated with purple and pink crepe paper and balloons. With purple and pink markers, Joey had lettered a big banner that read, "Happy Number Ten, Stef." The banner was draped over the fireplace.

The couch and chairs had been pushed against the walls and the rug had been rolled up to make a dance floor. The girls were dancing together, while the boys huddled around the refreshments table, throwing chips at each other.

Joey was up on the stairway landing, acting as disc jockey. He had a CD player, a stack of CDs, and a microphone.

Davey Chu was the last guest to arrive. When Jesse let him in, he walked straight over to Stephanie and handed her a gift.

"Sorry I'm late," he said, "but my mom was testing me on eleven-letter spelling words. Are you ready for tomorrow's spelling bee?"

"I sure am," Stephanie said confidently. "I've got a secret weapon."

"Oh yeah? What is it?"

Stephanie shrugged. "If I told you, it wouldn't be a secret." She wasn't about to explain a mnemonic device to her main rival.

They were interrupted by a "Yo, yo, yo!" Joey spoke into the microphone. "This is Joey Joe Badstone here at Stephanie's tenth birth-day party, pumping up the jams and jamming up the pumps. You know what I'm saying? I hope you do 'cause I don't have a clue. Okay, everybody—*party!*"

Jesse looked over at the group of boys huddled together. "Don't worry, Stef," he said. "I'll handle this." He went over to the group of boys.

"Okay, men, listen up." The group crowded around Jesse.

"It's perfectly normal to be shy around girls," he said. "You wonder if you're over-moussed or under-deodorized. I know how you feel."

One of the boys stared at him in disbelief. How could Stephanie's Uncle Jesse, with his dark, wavy hair and star's good looks know how they felt? "You mean *you* were shy around girls?" the boy asked.

Jesse looked at him as if he were crazy. "Of course not! You think I was some kind of nerd? And don't you be, either. Go dance with those girls."

The boys shrank back and made faces. "Eeeew," some of them said. "No way!" said others.

Jesse tried another approach. He went over to the girls.

"Okay, girls, this one's ladies' choice. Grab your favorite guy and go for it!"

The girls grabbed their favorite guy, all right. It was Jesse. They tried to drag him out onto the dance floor.

"Whoa, whoa, whoa!" Jesse called out, digging his heels into the floor. "Not me. I'm talking about those guys." He pointed toward the group.

Meanwhile, in the kitchen, Danny was putting candles on the birthday cake when D.J. and Kimmy came in through the back door. Danny looked up from the cake, and his jaw dropped. Kimmy had decided to go with the two-tone look, wearing the long blond wig on top of her newly dyed hair. Flame red curls burst out from the edges of the wig to frame her grinning face. She also wore a black jumpsuit and heels. And D.J., his own daughter, wore a pair of gold and black polka-dot leggings and a gold tunic. To Danny, she looked—well, he hated to think it—grown up. Both girls wore too much makeup, but this was no time to play Makeup Police.

"Hello, ladies," Danny said. "You're just in time to help with the party."

Kimmy looked around. "So where's Tommy Weaver? Tell him I'm here to fulfill his every wish."

Danny gave D.J. a stern look. "D.J., why did you tell Kimmy that Tommy was coming?"

D.J. shrugged. "Because I tell Kimmy everything."

"Okay then, tell her to go home."

"No can do, Mr. T.," said Kimmy. "I saw Tommy's limo outside. Now where are you hiding that awesome, adorable guy?"

Realizing he was in a no-win situation, Danny confessed. "He's waiting downstairs."

Kimmy bolted for the stairs to the basement.

"Freeze, Gibbler!" Danny said. "I need him in one piece. You girls go out and tell Jesse and Joey we're ready. And Kimmy, please don't do anything to embarrass us."

"I'll be the perfect lady . . . until I see Tommy. Then you'll have to hose me down!"

D.J. and Kimmy went into the living room, where the girls were still dancing with the girls and the boys were still hanging out with Jesse.

D.J. climbed the stairs to the landing, where Joey was playing the CDs. "He's ready," she whispered in Joey's ear.

Joey nodded and stopped the music. He signaled to Jesse, who crossed to where he had set up his electronic keyboard and the sheet music Tommy had given him earlier.

Danny came up to the landing and took the microphone from Joey. Before speaking into it, he quietly asked D.J. to go downstairs and move a chair into the center of the room.

D.J.'s heart was pounding as she stood in the center of the room. The big moment was about to happen. It would be the thrill of Stephanie's lifetime. Actually, it would be the thrill of her *own* lifetime.

Danny spoke into the microphone. "Everybody, please move back. Stephanie, please have a seat in the chair next to D.J." He came downstairs still holding the microphone.

Stephanie looked puzzled, but she went

over to the chair, sat down, and smoothed the ruffles on her party skirt. She had wanted to wear D.J.'s lime-green bicycle shorts to look cool and funky. But everyone had talked her into dressing up for the occasion. So she wore a hot pink Spandex top with a short ruffled blue and black skirt with big pink splashy flowers.

As Stephanie sat waiting, she had no idea what was coming. In the excitement of getting ready for her party, she had even forgotten—very briefly—about Tommy.

"Sweetheart," her father's voice boomed over the microphone. "This is a special gift from me to you."

"A chair?" Stephanie asked.

"A chair is just the beginning."

"Happy tenth birthday, honey. Hit it, Jess." Danny pointed at Jesse.

Jesse played a few opening chords as Tommy Weaver, America's reigning prince of rock-and-roll himself, entered from the kitchen and took the microphone from Danny.

Stephanie stood up and screamed. She couldn't believe her eyes. "Tommy Weaver!"

she cried. Dizzy with excitement, she sat back down again.

The other girls screamed. Even the boys screamed. But no one screamed louder than Kimmy, who made a lunge for Tommy. Luckily, D.J. was there to hold her back by the collar of her jumpsuit.

Tommy knelt on one knee in front of Stephanie and, looking deep into her eyes, began singing . . . a love song! It was one she had never heard before. "'Stephanie, how I wish that I could hold you in my arms forever, for eternity, Stephanie. Oh, Stephanie . . . Happy birthday, Stephanie."

Stephanie could hardly believe her ears. He had written a song just for her! Being ten was much better than being nine. She was glad she had worn the more glamorous outfit.

But like all songs, this song had an end. As Tommy finished singing, the others screamed and clapped, but Stephanie just stared at him with tears in her eyes.

"Thanks," she said, in a choked voice. That was all she could manage to say. Then she got up and gave her father the humungous hug he so richly deserved. What a dad!

"Happy birthday, honey," her father whispered.

"Dad, he's the best birthday present ever. Can I keep him?"

"That's funny, Stef," Danny said. But seeing his daughter's expression worried him. She wasn't kidding!

On the other side of the room, D.J. and Kimmy were still battling it out. "You can let go of me now, Deej," Kimmy pleaded helplessly. "I'll be cool—I promise."

The minute D.J. released her grip on Kimmy's jumpsuit collar, Kimmy rushed right over to Tommy and jumped into his arms.

"Hello," said Tommy, startled but polite. It wasn't every day he found a creature in a black jumpsuit, not to mention a platinum-blond wig with red curls poking out, suddenly sitting in his arms.

"I'm Stephanie's best friend, Kimberly Gibbler," said Kimmy. "Could I have your autograph? Just write, 'To Kimmy, the woman of my dreams.'"

"He writes music, not science fiction," Danny said, overhearing her.

Tommy set Kimmy down gently. "It's no problem," he said sweetly. "What would you like me to sign?"

"Here," said Kimmy, slipping off her shoe and holding out her foot. "Autograph this."

Grossed out, the other kids backed away. Danny and Joey closed in on Kimmy and picked her up.

"Wait," she cried, "he didn't sign my foot yet!" Ignoring her outburst, the two guys carried her off to the kitchen.

"I never saw that woman before in my life, Tommy," said Stephanie, pointing toward Kimmy. Then, grinning happily, she said, "Thanks *so* much for coming. Would you sign my CD?"

"Sure. You're the birthday girl," he said.

Stephanie ran up to her room to get the CD. While she was gone, Michelle came over to Tommy. "Hi, Tommy. My name is Michelle. You look almost as handsome as the Frog Prince."

"Thanks, Michelle."

"My birthday's in November. Start working on my song," she ordered him. Then she marched off to attack the birthday cake.

D.J., who'd been standing off to the side, finally saw her chance. Getting up her courage, she wandered over to Tommy, who was now standing alone. He looked even more handsome in person than he did in pictures . . . with wavy golden hair and dreamy blue eyes. Her heart was beating a mile a minute. As casually as she could manage, she said, "Hi, I'm Stephanie's big sister, D.J. Is this your first time in San Francisco?"

"Yeah, but I haven't had time to see anything," he said. His deep speaking voice was even better than his singing voice.

"Well, you've gotta go to Chinatown and Fisherman's Wharf," she said.

"Maybe you could show me around tomorrow?"

D.J. pointed at herself. "Me? I'd love to! Actually, I have to be in school tomorrow, but we just happen to have a half day off the day after tomorrow for teachers' conferences. How's Thursday?"

"Thursday afternoon would be great," said Tommy.

Was she really hearing this? Had Tommy Weaver actually asked her out on an honest-to-goodness date? What was she going to wear? How was she going to do her hair? Wait till she told Gibbler!

At that moment, Stephanie rushed downstairs with the CD. "I'm back," she said breathlessly. "Sorry I took so long."

D.J. stood back and gagged. "Stef, how many gallons of perfume did you put on while you were upstairs?"

"I just put on one little dab . . . from every bottle on your dresser." She turned to Tommy "Can you please sign this? I'll treasure it forever."

"Sure," he said.

She watched with a pounding heart as he signed her CD: "With all my love, Tommy."

SEVEN

The school auditorium was filling up fast with teachers, students, the principal, and the parents of the four spelling bee contestants.

From the end of her birthday party until now, Stephanie had thought of only two things—spelling and Tommy Weaver. She had practiced her spelling almost nonstop—except, of course, to sleep. Those mnemonic devices were really helpful. "Double the *c*, double the s: *s-u-c-c-e-s-s* . . . *success!*" Saying it over and over made her feel very confident. When the spelling bee was over, she could have all the time in the world to think about Tommy.

Danny was glad that he *didn't* have to think about Tommy. Now that his daughters had finally met the rock-and-roll star, they had stopped bothering Danny. Now he could just concentrate on watching Stephanie in the spelling bee.

Danny and Jesse were already in their seats when Joey raced in with Mr. Woodchuck, the dummy he used on his comedy show for kids.

"Here comes Stephanie," Danny whispered. "Doesn't she look smart?" He focused the camera on his daughter as she came onstage. She was followed by Davey Chu and the other fourth-grade spelling bee participants.

"She sure does look smart," said Joey.

"Intelligence runs in the family," Danny said as he snapped a picture.

"It must have skipped a generation," Jesse muttered. "Your lens cap is still on."

Onstage, Stephanie leaned over and whispered to Davey Chu, who sat next to her.

"You're going down, Chu. And it's all thanks to two little words . . . *mnemonic device.*"

"Dream on, Tanner," Davey whispered back. "They don't call me the human dictionary because I'm good at kickball."

Just then, Mr. Lowry, their teacher, stepped up to the podium. "Good afternoon parents, students, and friends. Welcome to the fourth-grade spelling championship. I'd like to introduce the top spellers in the fourth grade: Frannie Weisberg . . . Randy Gaines . . . Davey Chu . . . and our first speller today, Stephanie Tanner."

Joey, Danny, and Jesse cheered loudly as Stephanie stood up and went to the microphone.

"Stephanie," Mr. Lowry said, "your first word is *mnemonic.*

Stephanie's eyes lit up. "*Mnemonic?* Then a look of panic crossed her face. "*Mnemonic?* Uhm. Would you please repeat the word?"

"The word," Mr. Lowry said patiently, "is *mnemonic.*"

"And a very fine word it is," said Stephanie, stalling for time. "*Mnemonic.* A device or trick to help you remember things. *Mnemonic*."

"Stephanie," said Mr. Lowry, "this is not a definition bee. I need the spelling."

"Spelling? Oh, I'll give you spelling. *Rhododendron: r-h-o-d-o-d-e-n-d-r-o-n, rhododendron*."

"You have ten seconds to spell *mnemonic*, Stephanie."

In the audience, Joey and Jesse grabbed hold of Danny's arms nervously. Was their little girl going to make it?

Stephanie took a deep, shaky breath. "*Mnemonic: n-e-m-o-n-i-c . . . mnemonic*."

Joey, Jesse, and Danny all leaped to their feet and cheered. "All *right!*" When they saw everyone staring at them they sat down sheepishly.

"I'm sorry, Stephanie," said Mr. Lowry. "But that's incorrect."

Stephanie's expression crumbled.

"The next speller is Davey Chu."

Davey Chu stepped up to the microphone confidently. "*Mnemonic*," he said, "*m-n-e-m-o-n-i-c*."

"Correct," said Mr. Lowry.

The audience, with the exception of Stephanie's cheering squad, clapped.

"That eliminates Stephanie Tanner. Thank you, Stephanie," said Mr. Lowry.

"What? That's it? I did all that studying for one lousy word?" said Stephanie. "Come on, have a heart!"

"Do over!" Jesse muttered. Danny and Joey joined in, chanting, "Do over! Do over!"

"Just give me one more chance, please?" Stephanie begged. "Any other word. Any other word!"

"I'm sorry, Stephanie, you can take your seat with the rest of the class," Mr. Lowry said kindly.

Defeated, Stephanie dragged herself offstage and plopped down in the audience next to Jesse.

"The next speller is Randy Gaines," continued Mr. Lowry. "Randy, your first word is *incandescent*."

Stephanie jumped up, climbed onto the stage, and ran to the microphone. Grabbing it, she blurted out, "*Incandescent? I-n-c-a-n-d-e-s-c-e-n-t, incandescent*."

"Stephanie," Mr. Lowry said as gently as he could. "You have already been eliminated."

"*Eliminated?*" Stephanie repeated pitifully. "*E-l-i-m-i-n-a-t-e-d, eliminated.*"

That's when Danny, Jesse, and Joey got up and came onstage. They lifted Stephanie by the elbows and carried her off.

Back at the house, Rebecca had just finished feeding the twins. She yawned. They were teething, and she had been up most of the night with them.

Rebecca took off their bibs, which were completely covered with baby food, and said, "Gee, I could stick these in the fridge and have your lunch for tomorrow."

Just then, Danny, Jesse, Joey, and Stephanie trudged in through the back door.

"Hey, Rebecca," the guys greeted her halfheartedly. "Hey, Alex. Hey, Nicky," said Jesse. He went over and kissed the twins.

From the look on everyone's face, Rebecca was almost afraid to ask: "How'd you do, Stef?"

"How'd I do?" Stephanie repeated. "I missed on my first word. Not just on my first word, but the first *letter* of the first word."

Danny said, "We're very proud of Stephanie. There's nothing wrong with coming in fourth."

"Out of four? That's last, Dad. Last! Last! Last!" she said tearfully.

"C'mon, Stef," Joey said. "Who in the world knew *mnemonic* started with *m*?"

"Davey Chu," Jesse pointed out. But seeing Stephanie's miserable expression made him sorry he'd said it.

"I must have said *mnemonic* a hundred times," Stephanie said. "But did anyone ever ask me to spell it? Noooo. It's the stupidest word in the dictionary. Who is this Webster guy, anyhow?"

"Now, honey," her father said. "It's not fair to blame Mr. Webster. He didn't make up the words. He just listed them alphabetically."

"Well, I hate him anyway and I hate that Davey Chu." She stormed through the swinging door into the living room and flopped onto the couch.

Danny followed her in and sat beside her.

"No one likes to lose, Stef, but everybody loses sometimes."

"I want to be the best speller," Stephanie said, pounding her knee.

"You *are*. You're the best speller in your class. In fact, you might be the best speller in this house."

She looked at him. "Come *on*," she said.

"Okay," Danny admitted, "you *are* the best speller in this house, and you should be proud of your accomplishments. But no matter how great you are at something, there will always be a Davey Chu out there who might be just a little bit better. You're probably better at some things than Davey is."

"I guess I am a better dancer than he is."

"See? Anyway, it's just as important to be a good loser as it is to be a good winner."

Stephanie sighed and relaxed her shoulders. "You're right. I'm sorry. It's just that—" She broke off.

"What is it, honey?" Danny asked.

"It's just that, so far," she continued in a tight voice, "being ten hasn't been very much fun at all."

Danny gazed at Stephanie's gloomy face and said, "Honey, I promised Uncle Jesse I wouldn't tell you this, but you look like you could use some good news."

"What news?" Stephanie asked, showing only a slight interest.

"Tommy Weaver's coming over tomorrow to make a tape of your birthday song. Uncle Jesse's recording—"

"Tommy Weaver is taping my love song? Tomorrow?"

"He sure is," said Danny, relieved to see his ten-year-old daughter happy again.

EIGHT

The next day, just before dinner, Stephanie was sitting at the kitchen table with a pencil and notepad. She was doing her best to keep busy before Tommy came over to tape her song. Keeping busy always made the time go by faster.

"Comet, which sounds better?" she said dreamily. "Mrs. Tommy Weaver? Stephanie Weaver? Stephanie Tanner Weaver? Mrs. Stephanie Judith Tanner Weaver?"

Comet rolled over and offered his belly for a rub.

"No, you don't get a belly rub until we decide what's going on those wedding invitations," Stephanie said. She was sure Tommy felt the same way about her as she did about him. After all, he was coming over to tape her song—that *must* mean something. She was about to write "Stephanie Judith Weaver" when the pencil fell. She crawled under the table to get it.

At that very moment, the back door swung open, and in came her sister D.J.—with Tommy Weaver! Stephanie stayed crouched beneath the table so they wouldn't see her.

D.J. was saying, "Thanks for a great afternoon, Tommy. I never ate tacos in a limo before. Actually, I've never been in a limo before."

"I kinda guessed that," Tommy said, "when you went to sit up front with the chauffeur." They laughed.

"Well, Jesse's waiting for me downstairs in the studio," Tommy said. "I promised I'd make a tape of Stephanie's birthday song."

"I want to thank you for being so nice to

my sister," said D.J. "You've really brightened that child's *drab* little life."

Beneath the table, Stephanie scowled. She
felt like biting her sister on the ankle! But even
Comet couldn't get away with something that
drastic.

"It's my pleasure, D.J.," Tommy said.

Stephanie stared as Tommy leaned over and
kissed D.J. on the cheek.

D.J. stood there, lovestruck, as Tommy
headed downstairs to the studio. Slowly, she
raised a hand and touched the spot on her
cheek where he had kissed her.

"Yes!" She pumped her fist into the air, full
force.

Stephanie waited until D.J. had gone into
the living room. Then she came out from
under the table and, forgetting about the
dropped pencil, ran upstairs to her bedroom.
She flopped onto her bed and burst into tears.
How *could* she? How could her own sister do
this to her?

NINE

A few minutes later, after drying her tears, Stephanie went looking for Rebecca. She found her aunt up in the attic, changing Nicky's diaper.

"*Mama*. Say *mama*, Nicky," said Rebecca, leaning over the changing table. She looked up when she saw Stephanie. "I'm trying to teach him his first word," she explained to Stephanie. "Say *mama*, Nicholas."

Nicky giggled and drooled.

"Aunt Becky," Stephanie said, "can we talk, woman-to-woman?"

Rebecca finished diapering Nicky and lifted him off the table. "Sure, but I thought you'd be down in the studio, watching Tommy record your song."

"This is more important," Stephanie said. "Becky, what would you do if another woman stole Uncle Jesse from you?"

Rebecca smiled sweetly. "That would never happen because your Uncle Jesse and I have a loving and committed relationship based on mutual trust and respect. . . ." Suddenly, her expression changed. "The woman would never know what hit her," she added with a wicked grin.

Stephanie nodded. "Got it. She's toast. Thanks, Aunt Becky." She started to go back downstairs.

"Wait a minute," Rebecca said. "Is this about a boy at your party?"

Stephanie nodded. "You might say that. He really liked me, but another girl stole him right out from under my nose. The thief!"

"So who is this thief?" Becky wanted to know.

"Well, she was like a sister to me . . . but not anymore. I'm gonna win him back."

"Well, there's nothing wrong with letting him know why you're the one he should be with."

"Right. And if that doesn't work . . . she's toast!"

While Stephanie was talking to Rebecca, D.J. was at the top of the basement stairs, watching the studio light like a hawk. The light was red, which meant a recording session was under way and no one was allowed to go in. As soon as it was off, she could see Tommy again.

Just then, Kimmy barged in through the back door. "I know he's here. Where'd you stash him?" she said, looking around.

D.J. sighed. "Tommy's in the studio recording."

"Let's go!" Kimmy grabbed D.J.'s arm and started down the stairs.

D.J. pulled back. "You know the rules, Kimmy. We can't go down till the red light's off."

"All right, Tanner, " Kimmy said. "I want

details. What happened today with you and Tommy?"

"Before or after he kissed me?" D.J. said casually.

"*No!* You were actually kissing Mr. Awesome? I'm so happy for you." She whipped out her lip gloss and began to slather it on. "Mind if I take a crack at him?"

"*Yes*, I mind," D.J. said. "He's not running a kissing booth. Tommy and I are starting a real relationship."

"Hey, it was worth a shot." Kimmy shrugged. "Well, good luck, Deej. When the red light goes on, it's a green light for love, huh. See you later. I'm gonna check out my mother's closet—to see if she has a dress I can borrow to wear as your bridesmaid." And seconds later, Kimmy was gone.

TEN

Inside the studio, Jesse was working the soundboard as Tommy sat inside the booth singing to the track. The two of them had been down there for over an hour.

"Cut! That was great," Jesse yelled above the fading music. Tommy took off his headphones and stepped out of the booth.

"It was really nice of you to write that song just for Stephanie," Jesse said. He rewound the tape as he talked.

"Thanks, Jess," said Tommy, "but I gotta be honest with you. I wrote it for my girlfriend, Melanie. I just changed all the Melanies to Stephanies."

Jesse grinned. "Do us all a big favor and don't mention that to Stephanie."

Tommy grinned back. "Do me a favor. Don't mention that to Melanie."

Jesse switched off the red light. The session was over.

Just then, D.J. rushed in.

"Hi, I just happened to see the red light go off . . . not that I was like . . . waiting for the red light to go off because I do have a life . . . but since the red light did go off I thought I'd just come down and see why it went off. Oh, hi, Tommy," she finished breathlessly.

"Hey, Deej," Jesse said.

D.J. didn't even look at him. She only had eyes for Tommy.

Stephanie came in next, carrying a shoe box.

"Oh, hi, Tommy," Stephanie said as casually as she could manage.

"Hey, Stef," Jesse said. He got no response

from this niece either. "What am I, the Invisible Uncle?" he said, feeling left out. "Tommy, I'm gonna go get something to drink. What would you like?"

D.J. and Stephanie, who knew all about Tommy's likes and dislikes from the fan magazines, chimed in: "Iced tea, lemon, no sugar."

Jesse rolled his eyes and left to fill the order.

"I got the party pictures back, Tommy," Stephanie said when her uncle had gone. "Here's a nice one of us—suitable for framing." She handed Tommy a photograph of the two of them eating birthday cake.

D.J. was annoyed. Stephanie could be such a pest! It was Thursday and Tommy was leaving town tomorrow night. This might be her last chance to be alone with him. They had important things to discuss—whether they'd call or write letters, when he'd be in San Francisco again . . . everyone said long-distance relationships could be tough. She did not want or need a little sister to be her chaperon.

"Stef," D.J. said, "don't you have something to do? Like play with your Barbie doll or jump rope?"

"Don't you worry your pretty little pointed head about me," Stephanie said to D.J. She took another photograph out of the shoe box. "Oh, look at this one. We're dancing. Don't we make a cute couple?"

"Stef, Tommy doesn't want to look at pictures of some ten-year-old's birthday party."

Sensing the friction between the sisters, Tommy tried to smooth things over. "It's okay," he said. "I don't mind."

"No, D.J.'s right," Stephanie said with a resigned sigh. "You'd probably rather look at pictures of *her*. Which I just happen to have with me."

"What pictures?" D.J. asked, narrowing her eyes.

Stephanie dug a few more photographs out of the shoe box. They were much older than the first two. "Here's one of D.J. when she had the mumps. Doesn't she remind you of Mr. Potato Head?"

"Give me that!" D.J. grabbed the photograph and stuffed it into her pocket. She'd been six years old, and swollen as a grapefruit.

Before D.J. could stop her, Stephanie was already showing Tommy another picture. "Here's my personal favorite," she said. "Who could forget little D.J.'s first bath? Doesn't she have the cutest body? It's sort of like a mini-sumo wrestler. Did they have Baby Weight Watchers in those days? I guess not. Too bad."

D.J. smiled grimly at her little sister. "You're dead," she informed her.

"Look at this one. You can see the little rash on her little fanny. Did I say *little?* Silly me."

D.J. grabbed the picture, blushing crimson. "That's it! Excuse us, I'd like to have a little chat with my baby sister . . . *upstairs.*"

"Baby doesn't feel like chatting," Stephanie said.

"I do," D.J. said, grabbing her sister by the scruff of her neck. "Now!" She started shoving Stephanie up the stairs to the kitchen.

Over her shoulder, Stephanie sang out: "Tommy, I'll be right back!"

"No she won't," D.J. said between her teeth. "I promise."

When they reached the kitchen, D.J. spun

Stephanie around to face her. "How could you do this to me?"

"What about what you did to me, you back-stabbing, boyfriend-stealing traitor!"

"What? You actually think Tommy was your boyfriend? You're dreaming!"

"He was too my boyfriend."

Jesse put down the iced-tea pitcher and came over as referee. "Girls, girls. . . ."

The girls ignored him.

"And he's gonna dump you and come back to me after he finds out you drool in your sleep," Stephanie said.

"I do not!" D.J. sputtered.

"Yes you do! And I have the pictures to prove it."

She held up another photograph. D.J. tried to grab it but missed.

"Girls!" Jesse said again.

"Where did you get that?" D.J. cried.

"I took it while you were sleeping. I knew it would come in handy someday."

D.J. ran after her. "Give me that, you little worm."

The girls chased each other around and around the kitchen table. Jesse joined in, trying to catch either girl, but they were too fast for him. Finally, Stephanie headed through the swinging door to the living room. D.J. followed. Then came Jesse.

Danny and Joey were sitting on the couch with Michelle. They looked up as the three ran past them, circled around behind the couch, and dashed back into the kitchen again.

"What was that all about?" Joey asked.

"I don't know," Danny said, "but I'm about to find out."

ELEVEN

When the girls were on their third lap around the kitchen table, Jesse fooled them and switched directions suddenly. He grabbed Stephanie's arm, snatched the picture away from her, and held it high over his head. D.J. and Stephanie jumped up and down, trying to grab it.

"All right," said Danny, coming into the kitchen. "What's going on?"

"Next time you bring a star home, try

Mister Rogers," Jesse said to his brother-in-law.

"Stephanie thinks Tommy was her boyfriend, and she's showing him embarrassing pictures of me," D.J. said.

"He *was* my boyfriend till you stole him." Stephanie scowled at D.J.

"You're insane!" D.J. snapped.

"I am not insane! He signed my CD 'With all my love, Tommy,' didn't he?"

Just then, Joey walked in. "Stef, he signed *my* CD 'With all my love, Tommy,' too," he said.

"But he wrote a special song for me and he kissed me," said Stephanie. "I love him and he loves me."

"Honey," Danny said carefully, "I know you feel very strongly about this and I don't mean to hurt your feelings, but this isn't real love—it's just a crush."

"Your dad's right," Jesse said. He remembered the little talk he'd had with Tommy about his girlfriend, Melanie. Maybe he should tell Stephanie about Melanie. Maybe it would be better for her to know that Tommy hadn't written that song for her. But he couldn't do it. It would only make her feel worse. Instead, he said: "Stef, what you feel right now isn't really love. When you really fall in love, believe me, you'll know it."

"We know what you're going through, Stef," Joey said. "Sometimes you wish for something so bad you really start to believe it."

"Stef, you gotta face reality," said D.J., joining in. "Tommy was just being nice. He's not in love with you. He's in love with me."

At that, the three guys turned to stare at D.J. Clearly, Stephanie didn't have the only case of infatuation in the house.

"Deej," Danny said. "How can you be in love? You just met the guy."

"I know I only spent a couple of hours with him and it's true we haven't talked about a commitment yet, but it's getting pretty serious."

"Remember the nice talk we just had with Stephanie?" Danny said. "Well now we're gonna have it with you."

"Dad, she's a child; I'm a woman."

Danny looked worried. "Oh, I hope not! Not yet, please!"

Just then, Tommy peered around the corner from the basement stairs.

"Is it safe to come up yet?"

"Tommy, could you please straighten everybody out about what's going on between us?" D.J. said.

"Uh, well," Tommy said a little uneasily, "D.J. and I had a fun day and I hope we can be good friends."

D.J. stared at him in astonishment. "Friends? You mean like, *just* friends?"

"Yeah, I'm sorry if you misunderstood."

"Well, now that she's out of the way, I guess it's you and me, Thomas," Stephanie said smugly. She crossed through the center of the group to stand next to Tommy.

"Stephanie," Tommy said gently, "I want to be friends with you, too."

"You mean 'friends' like you're '*just* friends' with D.J.?"

He nodded. "I didn't mean to cause any trouble. I'm really sorry." Tommy put on his jacket. "I'd better get back to my hotel room so I can shower and grab a bite to eat before tonight's rehearsal. We're taping my next music video tonight."

Michelle rushed in from the living room. "Tommy, are you leaving?" she asked.

"Yeah." Tommy got down on one knee and gave her a peck on the cheek.

"You are such a babe," Michelle said, smiling.

"Thank you, Michelle. Good-bye. Good-bye, everybody."

Michelle turned around to her father. "Forget the Frog Prince! I know it sounds funny, Dad, but I think I'm gonna marry that guy."

Danny rolled his eyes to the ceiling. "It never ends."

TWELVE

Friday was a glum day. Everyone in the house was miserable. D.J. was mad at Stephanie and disappointed about Tommy. Stephanie was mad at D.J., crushed by her crush on Tommy, and still sad about losing the fourth-grade spelling bee. Rebecca and Jesse had gotten no sleep all week because the twins were teething. Joey had had a hard time with the kids on this week's show: ten criers, three wetters, and a kid who got a splinter on his bottom. Michelle's Frog Prince tape had broken. And Danny couldn't stand to see everyone so down.

Suddenly Danny had an idea—an idea so great that, if it worked, would surely qualify him for Father of the Year. Or, at the very least, Father of the Week. "All right, everybody, listen up," he said. "We're having a meeting in the living room!"

Everyone filed in obediently, but no one looked thrilled.

Danny took a deep breath and forged ahead. "If I didn't know any better, I'd swear this wasn't a happy family. Sure, you've had your share of disappointments. Sure, you've worked hard and didn't always come out on top. But that's no reason to be down in the dumps. I'm proposing that we all take a break from our troubles and go out to dinner. I hereby declare tonight Tanner Family Fun Night."

Danny looked around hopefully. His little pep talk wasn't exactly greeted by cheers. "C'mon you guys," he said enthusiastically.

"We're talking two hours of nonstop, laugh-filled, feel-good Tanner family fun. What do you say?"

This time, Joey, D.J., Stephanie, and Michelle grumbled and shrugged. "Yeah, why not?" they said. But they didn't sound too convincing.

"That's the spirit!" Danny clapped his hands. "Now go get your coats!" After the girls and Joey left the room, Danny turned to Rebecca and Jesse. "What are you guys waiting for? Tanner Family Fun awaits you, too! Suit up the twins and join us!"

"Sounds great," Jesse said dully.

"But we'll pass," Rebecca said. "We're all pretty wiped out tonight."

"Are you sure? We're gonna sing show tunes all the way there."

"Well, when you put it that way," Jesse said, forcing a smile, "we'll definitely stay home."

"Go ahead," Danny said, "miss the by-jingo jolliest night of the year."

Joey and the girls came back with their coats. Joey had changed from his Ranger uniform into jeans and a sweatshirt.

"Okay, troops, Tanner Family Fun Night is about to begin," said Danny. "Where should we go?"

"I want pizza," Joey said.

"I want burgers," D.J. said.

"I want tacos," Stephanie said.

"I need chocolate cake," Michelle said.

"Gee," Danny said, as he opened the door for them. "Too bad there's not an International House of Junk Food."

THIRTEEN

It was one of those family restaurants with a "fun" theme that wouldn't quit. The fun theme of this one was pirates.

As they walked in, Danny was still singing show tunes. D.J. had to reach over and tug on his sleeve to quiet him. "Dad, we're here. Please. People might hear you." She looked around, worried that someone she knew might actually be in this restaurant.

And what a restaurant! The waiters and

waitresses were dressed as pirates, in striped shirts, black hats with skulls and crossbones, and eye patches. In the center of the huge room was a life-size replica of a pirate ship, complete with a plank.

"Gee," Joey said, wryly, "it's all so authentic!"

"Authentically nerdy," Stephanie said.

A pirate sprang out in front of them. "Ahoy, you scurvy sea dogs! Welcome to ye Pirate Cove."

As they followed him through the large room to a table, they saw lots of fishing nets filled with plastic lobsters and starfish. Fake treasure maps hung on the walls.

Danny was really getting into the whole pirate theme. "Well, shiver me timbers," he exclaimed.

D.J. was not into it at all. "Dad, this place is so lame. What if my friends see me here?"

"Well, then, that would make them just as lame, wouldn't it? Yo-ho-ho, got you there, matey."

D.J. cringed and pulled her turtleneck sweater up over her nose.

Finally, when they reached their table, the

pirate waiter said, "All right. Slap your barnacles right here, mateys."

As they sat down, the waiter counted heads. "Okay, we have three Shipmates and two little Buccaneers." He handed large menus to Danny, Joey, and D.J., and kiddie menus to Stephanie and Michelle.

Stephanie held hers away from her. "I am ten years old now. A kiddie menu? For *moi?* How rude!"

"I'll tell you what rude is," D.J. said. "Rude is showing someone your sister's fat baby pictures! That's rude."

"Rude is calling your sister a worm the day after her birthday!" Stephanie said.

"Girls," Danny warned. "No squabbling allowed on Tanner Family Fun Night."

The two sisters glared at each other.

"Look!" said Michelle joyfully. She was pointing at her kiddie menu. "Puzzles!"

"Connect the dots," said Stephanie dryly. "Very challenging."

"Don't worry," Michelle said. "I'll help you."

Joey looked at the menu. "I'm not big on fish. You got any pizza here?"

"Arrrgh!" said the pirate. "Maybe you didn't notice the motif, pal, but there's kind of a seafood thing going on here. But I'll go up to the galley and try to drum up a sliver of dried salted beef."

"Yum," said Joey glumly.

The pirate walked away laughing.

"What a goofball," Stephanie commented.

"He's just doing his job, honey," Danny said. "Now come on, let's all get into the pirate spirit. And what better way than by wearing our cardboard pirate hats?" Danny put his on.

D.J. said, "Dad you look like a dweeb."

"Ah, but I'm a dweeb having fun because everything's more fun with a hat on. C'mon gang, put 'em on."

Reluctantly, they all put on their pirate hats. The pirate waiter returned.

"Are you swabbies ready to order?"

"Dad, please," Stephanie said, "please don't make me order from the kiddie menu."

"Okay, honey. It's Tanner Family Fun Night. You can have whatever you like." Danny swapped menus with her.

"I believe I'll have the Sunken Treasure."

Stephanie read from the grown-up menu: "'A scrumptious assortment of King Neptune's favorites from the bottom of the sea.'"

Danny approved. "Now *that* sounds like a fun meal." He looked at D.J.'s menu and found the item Stephanie had ordered. "For thirty-three dollars, it better be," he added under his breath.

"I believe I'll have the chocolate cake," Michelle said happily.

"Sorry, we're out," the waiter said.

"No chocolate cake? What a rip-off!"

"Everybody down!" D.J. cried out suddenly. "Get down, get down, get DOWN!" They all ducked under the table.

"Deej," Joey asked, "what's wrong?"

"There are some kids from my school sitting a few tables over."

"Oh yeah!" Danny got back up on his chair. He looked around until he saw them. "That's Shelley Phillips." He lifted an arm to wave. D.J. grabbed it just in time. If anybody from school saw her here, she'd die of embarrassment. Just die!

"Dad, please! Don't do anything to attract attention."

FOURTEEN

"Are my friends looking at me?" D.J. was trying her best to hide behind her hair. She ignored the food that the waiter had placed in front of her ten minutes before.

"Nobody's looking at you," Danny told her.

That wasn't exactly true. Shelley and her date and the couple they were with had noticed D.J. a few minutes before. Since then, they had done nothing but point at D.J. and whisper.

"Can I wait in the car?" D.J. asked miserably.

"There's no fun in the car," Danny said. "All the fun is right here."

In utter disgust, Stephanie dug into her Sunken Treasure with her fork. She came up with something gray and slimy with tentacles.

"Ugh," she said, "what the heck did I order? Here, Michelle." She flung the slimy thing onto her little sister's heap of fish and chips.

"Eeeew, gross! Kill it, Daddy!" Michelle passed it on to her father's bread plate.

"Honey, it's octopus and it's already dead." Danny picked it up and dropped it onto the tray of a passing busboy.

"Toss this one back in the tank," he said.

"Will you all please behave?" D.J. whispered furiously. As if it weren't bad enough that she had to be out with her family, they were behaving like a bunch of ill-mannered peasants.

Everyone was just about finished eating when Joey's order arrived.

"Ahoy," said the waiter, setting down the plate. "Knockwurst and potato pancakes for the landlubber."

"It's about time," Joey said.

D.J. felt someone tap her on the shoulder. She turned and gasped. There before her was Shelley Phillips, wearing a smirk on her face.

"Hi, D.J."

"Hi, Shelley." D.J. gulped. "What are you doing here?"

"I'm here with Brian, Jamie, and Andrew. We thought it would be a riot to come make fun of all the lame families that eat here."

"Yeah, that's why we're here, too," D.J. said, trying to sound as cool as Shelley even though she burned with shame.

"Uh-*uh*, it's Tanner Family Fun Night," Michelle informed Shelley before D.J. had a chance to clap a hand over her little mouth.

Shelley cracked up.

"Thanks, Michelle," D.J. said sarcastically.

"I gotta tell the guys this one," Shelley said before heading back to her table, laughing to herself.

"And I gotta find a new school," D.J. said faintly. Her life was over.

Stephanie fished up a new treat from her plate. This time, it was squid. "Eeew, this one has eyes. I can't eat anything that's looking at me!" She made a face and pushed her plate away.

Danny took her plate and put it in front of Joey. He was already almost finished with his kiddie portion of knockwurst and potato pancakes. "You can't waste all that food, Stef," Danny said. "Joey, you want some?"

Joey put up both hands. "Danny, that's not dinner, that's Marine Land." He pushed the plate back to Danny.

"I think I'm gonna be seasick," Stephanie said.

"A whole semester trying to be cool wiped out by one night of Tanner Family Fun," D.J. said bitterly.

"I know they have chocolate cake at the Sizzler," Michelle complained.

"That's it!" Danny pounded the table with his fist. "We're outta here. Check, please." He started to get up as their waiter approached.

"Not so fast, matey," the waiter said. "I spy a landlubber who didn't finish his Sunken Treasure. That means you walk the plank."

Suddenly, a spotlight shone on Danny. Bells went off. People started clapping and chanting: "Walk the plank, walk the plank, walk the plank." All eyes were on them. This was obviously part of the restaurant's fun pirate theme.

A couple of pirates approached and grabbed Danny by the arms. They led him off to the ship in the middle of the restaurant. The plank extended out over a big wooden tank, which was filled with brightly colored plastic balls.

"Plank! Plank! Plank!" their fellow diners chanted.

"Enough!" the head pirate shouted.

The crowd fell silent.

"Any last words?" the waiter asked Danny.

"Yes, there's something I'd like to say to my family. Tonight I had a dream that people who love each other could go out together— to laugh, to have fun, to eat fish."

D.J., Joey, Stephanie, and Michelle hung their heads in shame. He was right. They had not carried on like happy pirates tonight—far from it.

"But who am I kidding?" Danny went on. "Only myself. I'm ready now."

"Plank! Plank! Plank! Plank!" the crowd started up again.

Danny put one foot on the plank.

Just then, Stephanie ran up onto the ship. "Dad, wait! It's all my fault. I'm the one who ordered 'The Undersea World of Jacques Cousteau.' If anyone deserves to walk the plank, it's me."

"Plank! Plank! Plank!" the crowd chanted.

Danny and Stephanie were about to walk the plank together when Joey ran up. "No, Stef, I'm the one who should walk the plank. We didn't have fun because of my bad attitude. So they didn't have pizza. So what?"

"Wait for me!" Michelle scrambled up after them.

Finally, D.J. came up. "Joey's right, Dad. We all had bad attitudes. I'll admit, at first I was embarrassed to come here, but now that I'm standing on a boat and everybody's staring at me, I'm totally humiliated."

Danny smiled proudly. "Thanks for coming up here, guys. That's the kind of Tanner family togetherness I was hoping for."

"Plank! Plank! Plank!"

"All right, I'll walk the plank ... not

88

because I didn't clean my plate, but because I came here for Tanner Family Fun Night and doggone it, we Tanners are gonna have fun. Are you with me, buckos?"

Danny held his nose and took the plunge. "Geronimo!"

The crowd cheered.

"Well, blow me down. Whoa!" Joey said, in his best Popeye voice, and teetered over into the vat of plastic balls after Danny.

"It's my turn. Cowabunga!" said Michelle, following Joey.

Stephanie was just about to jump when D.J. grabbed her sleeve. "Before you jump, Stef, I'd like to say something to you."

"Yeah?" Stephanie said.

"I'd like to apologize for the way I've been treating you lately."

"You mean like a little worm?"

"Yeah. I guess I was really dumb. I mean, one innocent little kiss on the cheek and I thought Tommy and I were practically engaged!"

"*You're* dumb?" Stephanie said. "At least you didn't make up wedding invitations."

"I guess we were both pretty dumb," D.J.

said. "If I had known this was going to happen, I never would have asked Dad to invite Tommy Weaver to your birthday party."

"*You* asked him?" Stephanie was surprised. "I thought Dad came up with the idea himself."

"Are you kidding? Dad was afraid we'd be too much for Tommy. And I guess he was right."

"D.J., if Tommy was just a crush, I don't know if I'll be able to take it when the real thing happens," Stephanie said thoughtfully.

"I know what you mean," said D.J., nodding. "Hey, you know what I just realized? I'm standing here on the deck of this stupid pirate ship talking to you about boys and love. . . . Stef, you really *are* growing up."

"Well, being ten is a lot harder than being nine," Stephanie said. "I mean, my birthday was only three days ago, and I've already had my heart broken, lost the fourth-grade spelling bee, and embarrassed my sister in front of a rock star. I'm really sorry, Deej."

"It's okay. You know, one of these days, we'll both be dating like crazy."

"Yeah," said Stephanie thoughtfully. "I promise I won't try to steal any of your boyfriends."

"Same goes for me," said D.J., "because guys will come and go, but you and I will be sisters forever."

They hugged.

From the tank, Danny called up to them. "Hey, girls! What are you waiting for?"

"Come on in," Joey said. "The plastic's great!"

"Better than chocolate cake!" Michelle exclaimed.

Then together, D.J. and Stephanie screamed "Cowabunga!" and jumped off the plank to join the others in the vat of colorful plastic balls. Everybody squealed in delight, for Tanner Family Fun Night was just beginning.